THE ANTI-VIRAL ADVENTURES OF MAX AND MIA

In the bustling Body City, two of the bravest and most skilled Anti-viral detectives, Max and Mia Flublok, received a special assignment from their chief at the Microbial Police Department.

Their orders were clear: track down a dangerous fl u virus that had been causing chaos in the lungs district of the city. Max and Mia knew that this mission would be no easy feat.

Gathering their detective gear and supplies, Max and Mia set out on their mission, determined to put an end to the flu virus's rampage.

As they navigated through the bloodstream from MPD

headquarters they could see the lung district come into sight.

It wasn't long until they encountered a gang of cold viruses who had been sent to try and lead them astray and stop them getting vital information about the flu virus's whereabouts.

But Max and Mia were not about to give up that quick. With their quick thinking and bravery, they outsmarted the cold gang try to distract them and pressed on in their search.

Using all of their detective skills, they chased the flu virus, determined to bring it to justice. In the end, they emerged victorious, arresting the flu virus and delivering it to the Microbial Police Department, where it was locked away for good.

Max and Mia were hailed as heroes of the city. And from that day on, they continued to serve as anti-viral detectives, protecting the body from all kinds of dangers and solving mysteries with their courage and determination.

This story is dedicated to the two most amazing kiddos in the world, Roxy and Ruairi!

Just like Max and Mia, the brave detectives in this story, I hope you both never stop

being curious and adventurous. Dream big, work hard and don't give up. And

remember, no matter what, you'll always have someone to cheer you on! This story is

a special gift for you both, enjoy the adventure and have fun!

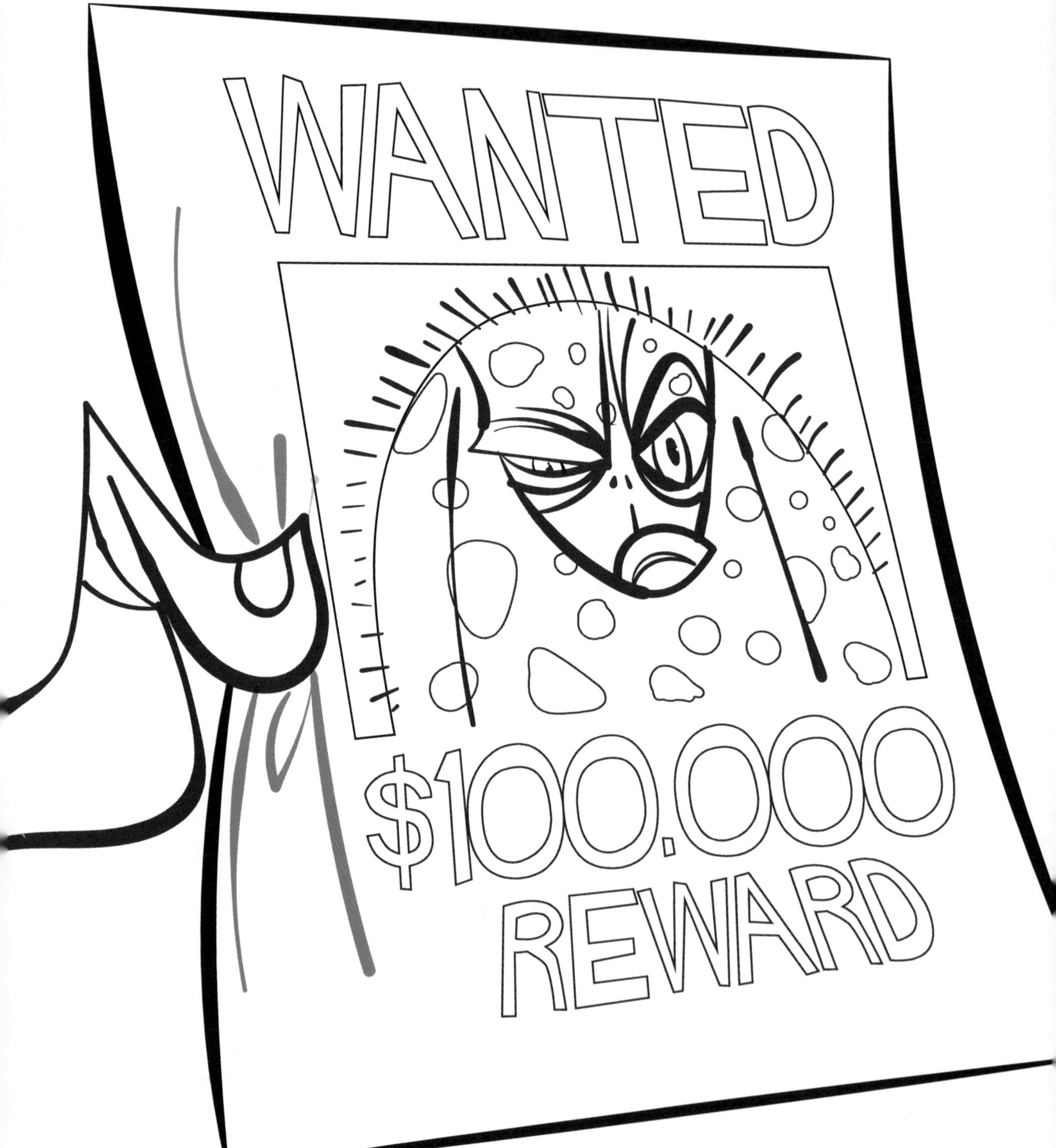
WANTED
$100,000
REWARD

Printed in Great Britain
by Amazon

25407003R00016